SULTAN
The Patient

Home Farm Twins

Sultan

The Patient

Jenny Oldfield

Illustrated by Kate Aldous

*Hodder
Children's
Books*

a division of Hodder Headline plc

A Catalogue record for this book is available from the British Library

ISBN 0 340 74394 8

Typeset by Avon Dataset Ltd, Bidford-on-Avon, Warks

Printed and bound in Great Britain by
The Guernsey Press Co. Ltd, Guernsey, Channel Islands

Hodder Children's Books
a division of Hodder Headline plc
338 Euston Road
London NW1 3BH

One

'Eggbutt snaffle!' Hannah Moore challenged. 'Vulcanite pelham!' She was riding Sultan, Laura Saunders' graceful chestnut thoroughbred.

'Browband, throatlash, cantle, gullet and stirrup bar!' Her twin sister, Helen, shouted back all the strange horsey words she could think of. She rode Solo, their own silver grey pony, easing him down the steep slope of Doveton Fell. They wanted both horses to be ready to tackle the Three Peaks Pony Trek this coming Saturday.

'Throat – what?' their father asked. He'd come

1

up the fell on foot to take photographs of the twins on horseback, bringing their Border collie, Speckle, and their mongrel, Scruffy, to race across the rocky hillside.

'Throatlash. It's part of a horse's bridle.'

Click-click – whirr! David Moore took a picture of Hannah struggling for control as the highly-strung Sultan came to a sudden stop. 'And what's an eggbutt whatsit?'

'Snaffle.' Helen eased Solo on with a quick, light squeeze of her legs. 'It's the metal part that goes into the horse's mouth.'

'Sounds like a cream-cake your mum might have on the menu at the Curlew!' Helen's dad caught her on camera sitting straight-backed, head held high. 'Since when did you two know so much about horses' tack?' he asked.

'Since Laura let us look after Sultan while she's away at school.' Hannah felt her horse jolt back into action down the stony track. 'You should see her tack room!'

The twins called on Sultan at Doveton Manor every day. 'She's got everything; bridle racks, a saddle horse, dandy-brushes, currycombs—' Helen gabbled through another list until David Moore broke in.

'Whoa! I'm blinded by science!' He moved in to take a close-up of Sultan's elegant face and big brown eyes. 'So, who do we like best; this beautiful, exotic creature, or good old Solo?'

'Not fair!' Hannah protested. From under the peak of her hard hat she could see Speckle and Scruffy making a lightning dash up the hill towards them, their long coats streaming in the wind. 'You can't compare them!'

Sultan was 15 hands of well-bred, gleaming chestnut horseflesh, long-limbed and elegant; Solo was a dumpy 12.2 hands in his iron shoes. Sultan was five years old and in his prime; Solo was twelve, and long in the tooth.

'They're completely different,' Helen agreed. She made Solo wait on a flat stretch of track. You only had to give Solo a touch on the reins for him to do as he was told, whereas Sultan liked to argue. She watched him now as Hannah let him pick his own way down to the ledge, leaning forward in the saddle to pick out dangers on the way.

'Sultan has a mind of his own,' Hannah said.

'He thinks he's always in the right.'

'Bossy.'

'Vain.'

'But we love you all the same!' they said together.

Click-click! Mr Moore captured the two horses standing quietly, gazing down the fell. It was spring and the countryside was coming back to life after a long, cold winter. White blossom was out on the hawthorn trees, the grass in the narrow valley below was a fresh, bright green.

'And we love you too, Solo!' Helen reminded him. He fitted in perfectly at cosy, rundown Home Farm, whereas Sultan definitely belonged at Doveton Manor, the grandest house around. 'You're easy-going, and you never let us down. And on top of all that, you're very, *very* handsome!' She patted Solo's sturdy dappled neck and shoulders.

Up went the pony's ears, he gave a pleased snort and a flick of his long white tail.

Click – whirr – whirrr! The film came to an end.

'And a sucker for flattery!' the twins' dad teased

as they called it a day and headed for home.

'Anyway, it's not a competition,' Hannah pointed out later that night.

The twins were up in their bedroom, planning the weekend trek on Solo and Sultan. Speckle and Scruffy lay by Hannah's bed, tired after their long run on the fell, while Socks, their young tabby cat, lay curled on Helen's duvet in the last rays of the evening sun.

'I'm not saying it is,' Helen objected. For some reason, even after both horses were safely stabled for the night, the Sultan versus Solo debate niggled on. 'I'm just saying Solo never gives up. He sticks at things until he gets them right.'

'Whereas Sultan gives up?' Hannah frowned. She spread the map of Doveton and the sur-rounding fells on her bed, sat cross-legged, and began to mark a route in red felt-tip.

'I never said that either.' Helen shoved her dark hair behind her ears. 'But you just have to look at Solo to see he's strong.'

'You mean he's got short, stumpy legs.'

'No. I'm talking about his deep chest and broad

shoulders. They show he's got stamina.'

'And just because Sultan's tall and leggy, he hasn't?' Hannah knew that Laura's thoroughbred didn't have the same staying power as their own pony, but she wouldn't admit it. 'He'll show you who's got stamina on Saturday!' she promised. She finished drawing the red route on the map and pushed the top on to the pen.

'Three fells in one day; twenty-five miles, mostly uphill.' Helen chewed her lip. She wasn't sure if even gutsy little Solo could manage the course organised by the riding-school in nearby Nesfield for its annual spring trek.

'Yeah?' Hannah queried, uncrossing her legs and heading down the corridor to the bathroom. Down in the kitchen, the phone rang. 'We've had them in training for the last few weeks, haven't we? Slowly building up their strength. It's not like we're springing it on them.'

'Helen-Hannah!' their mum called from downstairs. 'It's Laura on the phone.'

'I'll get it.' Helen shot off her bed, disturbing the sleepy cat. 'Sorry, Socks! – Hi, Laura!' She was down the stairs and had grabbed the phone before Hannah got there. '. . . Yep, everything's fine, thanks. We took Sultan up Doveton Fell today.'

'Did he behave himself?' Laura Saunders was as anxious as ever about her beautiful but temperamental horse.

'Hannah was riding him. He walked through the village main street, no problem.'

'Didn't the cars bother him?'

'No. He's getting used to the traffic now.'

'How did he get on with Solo?'

'Great. He didn't try to nip or bite him, or anything like that.'

'Good. So you think you'll go ahead with the trek this weekend?'

'Probably. We've got our names down at the riding-school.' Helen hid her doubts. 'It'll be good exercise, good experience for him.'

'Well, just make sure he doesn't boss the other horses about too much.' On the other end of the phone line Laura sighed. It was only three weeks since she'd gone back to school after the Easter holidays, and three more until she came back to Doveton for half-term. 'And tell him I miss him,' she whispered.

*

'Come on, Sultan, you can do it!' It was Helen's turn to ride the thoroughbred. They were down by the lake, wading along the pebbly shore, except that Sultan had refused to go into the cold, clear water.

'Look, Solo doesn't mind getting wet!' Hannah showed him how it was done. It was Friday, the day before the trek. She knew that the Three Fells course would bring them along the water's edge and that the horses would probably jostle and crowd each other into the water. She let Solo surge knee-deep into the lake.

But Sultan was having none of it. Paddling was beneath him. He pulled at the reins and twisted away until Helen took a firm grip and steadied him. 'Don't be a spoilsport,' she soothed.

Gingerly the thoroughbred lifted a hoof and placed it in the water. Helen urged him on. She smiled at the dainty way he lifted his feet, while Solo splashed and trundled ahead. 'Good boy!' At least he was having a go.

'Solo loves it,' Hannah called. She felt the pony surge ahead, sending up glittering spray as he

broke into a trot. Two swans gliding towards the shore quickly changed course to get out of his way. Farther out, passengers in a tourist steamer leaned out to wave. Behind them, the far shore rose sheer to Hardstone Fell, one of the three peaks that they would climb the next day.

Sultan snorted. He pulled back and dawdled until Helen gave in and eased him back on to dry land, where his hooves clattered on the grey pebbles. 'I think I'll head back to the Manor with him,' she called. 'It's no good if he's not enjoying himself.'

'OK, see you there.' Hannah would join her later to help rub Sultan down and turn him out into the paddock. But for a while she would let Solo enjoy the fun.

So Helen and Sultan set off alone, trotting up the beach, then slowing to a walk along the long main street with its rows of neat slate houses, past Luke Martin's village shop with its white devecote, past Mr Winter's terraced house where his cairn terrier, Puppy, barked loudly through the gate.

'Yap-yap!' The terrier scurried back up the path,

took a run at the gate and launched himself at it.
It shook and rattled as his paws hit the latch.

Sultan skittered sideways into the road. Helen
steadied him. 'Take no notice, it's only Puppy,'
she muttered. The least little thing could upset
Sultan.

'Lucky there wasn't a car coming,' Luke Martin
remarked. He'd been on his way from the shop
to the cricket pitch down the road, but stood to
one side as the horse played up. 'He's a bit of a
handful, isn't he?'

'Sometimes. I think he's tired; that's why he's
edgy.' She was anxious to carry on, get Sultan
safely home and resting in his paddock. As Luke
went to calm Puppy down, she carried on down
the narrow street.

Doveton Manor was at the end of the village.
The turn-off up the drive came just after the
cricket pitch, and as soon as Sultan could see the
tall double gates of home, Helen knew he would
quicken his pace . . . but not before he had slowed
to a crawl to nip at the fresh hawthorn leaves of
the cricket pitch hedge, and to graze new grass
and wild flowers in the hedgerow.

Helen sighed and let him have his head. She heard Hannah come up from behind and pass them. The pony still had a spring in his step and a jaunty look in his eye.

'It's not a competition!' Helen remembered Hannah's words and sighed. As she urged the reluctant Sultan along the road home, she couldn't hide from herself a sneaking, secret feeling that if it did come to a contest between sturdy Solo and beautiful-but-difficult Sultan, in her book the pony would come out on top every time.

Two

Lady, the Saunders' Siamese cat, arched her back and hissed.

'It's OK, it's only me!' Hannah took off her hard hat and let her hair fall forward. 'See!'

It was early the next morning, the day of the Three Peaks Trek. She'd ridden her bike down from Home Farm to Doveton Manor ahead of Solo and Helen, to get Sultan ready.

Lady prowled round the edge of the fishpond, proud and sleek; in and out of Mrs Saunders' flower-pots and stone statues. When Hannah went to stroke her, she flicked her long black tail and stalked off.

'Hannah, or is it Helen? You're early.' Val Saunders, Laura's mother, peered out through the French windows, clutching the neck of her white satin dressing-gown. Her long blonde hair was down over her shoulders, her face scrubbed clean of its usual make-up. 'We haven't even had breakfast yet.'

'I'm Hannah. It's the trek today,' she reminded Mrs Saunders.

'Ah yes. Well, it's a lovely day, and I'm sure Sultan will be very pleased to see you. Without you twins, he wouldn't get nearly enough exercise!'

'Who's that we're talking about?' Another figure appeared in the doorway. 'Sultan? Quite right. He's lazy by nature, that horse. Thinks the world owes him a living.'

Hannah stepped back as Geoffrey Saunders came out on to the terrace. She was always a bit scared of Laura's father, who was tall and un-smiling, with a loud voice and brushed back grey hair. He was wearing a smart pullover and neatly pressed trousers.

'Good idea to get him out on this Three Peaks

14

business,' he told Hannah. 'Do him good. Took a look at him last night and thought he was putting on a bit of weight.'

'I'll just go and saddle him up then.' Hannah slid past the two grown-ups towards the stable yard. She would take the headcollar from the tack room and lead Sultan into the yard to get him ready.

Mr and Mrs Saunders followed at a distance, watching her climb the fence. For a few minutes Sultan sulked at the far side of the paddock, picking at the grass, until Hannah cornered him and slipped the collar over his ears.

'You don't think he looks a bit off-colour?' Mrs Saunders asked her husband as Hannah led him into the yard. The horse's head was down, his step heavy.

Mr Saunders grunted. 'Probably knows what's ahead of him, that's all.' He went and firmly patted the horse's neck. 'Doesn't fancy climbing three mountains in one day!'

'Perhaps it is too much.' Laura's mother was softer, more sympathetic than her father.

Hannah waited for them to make up their

minds. It was true; Sultan did look down in the dumps.

Just then Helen came trotting up the drive on Solo. The morning sun shone on his light grey, dappled coat, his brushed white mane and tail blew in the breeze. He arrived with a jaunty step, with Speckle and Scruffy running closely to heel. The dogs, too, were set for a day on the fells.

'If Solo can do it, I'm sure Sultan can!' Geoffrey Saunders decided. He turned to Hannah. 'Just keep his mind on the job,' he advised. 'I know he can be headstrong, so don't be afraid to be firm. And he's a bit lazy and out of condition lately, so don't let him lag behind to graze at the roadside. He's doing that at the moment, and it's a bad habit. You have to watch what he's eating.'

As she slung the saddle over Sultan's broad brown back, then tightened the girth strap, Hannah listened to the advice. 'He'll be OK once we get going,' she promised.

'Come on, we've only got an hour to get to Nesfield,' Helen insisted.

'We're coming.' Hannah slotted leather straps

through keeper rings and checked the stirrups. At last she was ready.

Eight o'clock on a bright, breezy spring morning. A blue sky with wispy white clouds. Three Lakeland peaks and a whole day ahead of them. She swung into the saddle with a leg-up from Mr Saunders, who gave Sultan a last, firm pat and sent them on their way.

'Have a good day!' Mrs Saunders cried, waving a slim hand.

Helen and Hannah waved back. Speckle and Scruffy tucked in behind Solo, and they were off.

There were cream ponies and black ponies, browns, bays and chestnuts crowding into the cobbled square. There were horses with white socks and faces, stripes, blazes and stars. Riders with short legs perched on fat ponies with wide backs, riders whose legs dangled from ponies they had long outgrown.

They all gathered to set off from Nesfield town square at nine o'clock, straggling down from the farms and out of the lakeside villages for the local newspapers to take their pictures and the local drivers to get furious at the traffic hold-ups that the spring event always created.

'There's Mum!' Helen spotted Mary Moore standing at her cafe door, her dark hair tied up, dressed in flowery trousers and T-shirt, with a big white apron tied round her middle. She let Scruffy and Speckle trot across to say hello, saw their mother come halfway to meet them.

'What's she bringing?' Hannah's eyes lit up as she noticed two small rucksacks.

'Sandwiches, cake and drinks!' Mary Moore declared.

Scruffy and Speckle wagged their tails excitedly at the smell of food from the bags. 'Not for you!' Mary laughed, handing them to the twins. 'It's going to be a long day, so make them last.'

'What kind of cake?' Helen asked.

'Home-made chocolate fudge.'

'Yum!' the twins said together, bending to take the bags and slipping their arms through the straps.

'And a few dog biscuits in a separate plastic bag,' their mum added, not forgetting Speckle and Scruffy. She showed the dogs their special treat.

The black and white collie and tousled fawn mongrel wriggled with delight.

At the head of the crowd of jostling ponies and horses, the riding-school instructor gave the order to begin.

'About time!' someone called from the queue of cars waiting to park in the square.

Mary Moore smiled up at the twins. 'Be careful,' she told them. 'Stick with the group, follow the proper route.'

'We will, Mum.' Helen let Solo slip eagerly into the procession, checked that the two dogs were following.

'And don't get lost!' their mum called, her voice tinged with worry.

'We won't!' Hannah waited for the end of the line, then steered Sultan after them. He fought for his head but she held firm. Today's the day, she told herself. If I don't show him who's boss on this trek, I might as well give in!

Solo loved the wind in his mane on the top of Doveton Fell. He trod surefootedly up the loose stone screes until he reached the ridge and looked back down Hardstone Pass to Nesfield, nestling on the edge of Rydal Lake, which gleamed silver under the sun.

'Well done!' Helen patted his neck and drew to one side to let the stragglers pass. These were the elderly, short-winded horses whose riders let them take things easily, or the small ponies plodding slowly up the steep, wild hill. Helen smiled and chatted as they passed. But behind her smile she was worried.

'Come on, Sultan!' she murmured. She could see him toiling up the hill, the very last straggler of all. Scruffy and Speckle had slowed to keep him company, cutting off across the hill after the scent of a rabbit, but always trotting patiently back to see how Sultan was getting along. Every step the horse took was unwilling, every toss of his head showed that he wished he was somewhere else. 'Is he OK?' Helen called to Hannah, as once more the thoroughbred stopped for a rest in the shade of a tall rock.

'He's sweating and breathing hard.' Hannah waited with a worried frown. 'It's not like him to be out of breath.'

Helen swung round in the saddle to look at the line of horses and riders strung out along the ridge of Doveton Fell. Ahead of them lay the steepest hill of all, up to the summit of High Peak, a jagged, tent-shaped mountain that would test the stamina of all who attempted it. She felt Solo itching to carry on and catch up with the others, but she made him wait for Sultan and Hannah.

At last Sultan made it to the ridge, with the two dogs walking quietly behind. 'Look at his neck; it's covered in sweat!' Hannah drew him up alongside Helen. A lather of sweat had collected along the underside of his graceful neck and across his withers. The cantle at the front of the saddle was stained dark, and Sultan's sides heaved from the effort of the climb.

'Watch out!' Helen cried as Sultan shifted sideways, tossing his head and stamping his feet. She had to move Solo smartly to one side. The grey pony only just held his footing on the narrow ridge. Speckle barked a short, sharp warning.

'Sorry!' Hannah tightened his reins. Sultan was even more restless than usual. His eyes rolled as he snorted and shook his head. 'Helen, I don't think he's just being awkward; I think there's something wrong with him!'

Helen felt a stab of panic in her chest. She drew a sharp breath. 'You mean he's sick?' She swung round to see how far behind the rest of the trekkers they were. Too far to shout a message that they were turning round and going back. Anyway, they were halfway round the course that led full-circle back to Nesfield. It would be as far to go back as it would be to go on.

'I'm not sure.' Hannah didn't want to jump to conclusions. 'Maybe he's just a bit out of condition, like Mr Saunders said.'

Sultan stamped and twisted his hindquarters sideways, spooking Solo, who edged out of his way.

'It looks worse than that.' Helen saw that he was dripping with sweat, and that his sides heaved in and out. 'Should we take him back?'

'What would Mr Saunders say?' Hannah didn't want to admit that Sultan hadn't finished the trek. She thought they should go on. 'Anyway, it wouldn't be any quicker.'

'But we've still got High Peak up ahead. That's the steepest part of all.'

'But that's where everyone else will be. If we go back, there'll be no one else around. And how would we let them know?' Hannah didn't want to be stranded and cut off from the main party. These fells were steep and wild, with only an occasional walker or a pair of mountain climbers passing every now and then. She remembered what their mum had said about sticking with the main group.

Helen nodded. 'Well, you're the one who's riding him. If you think he can make it—'

'Let's try!' But as Hannah tried to swing Sultan round to face along the ridge, he stamped and sent stones sliding towards the dogs. One sharp piece of slate caught Scruffy's leg, and the little mongrel dog yelped with pained surprise. He jumped up to escape the sliding avalanche and tangled himself among Solo's legs. The pony flinched, then barged clumsily ahead, coming up on Sultan from behind, so that the thoroughbred leaned back on his hindquarters and lifted his front hooves in the air.

'Steady!' Hannah cried. She clung on with her legs and held tight to the reins.

Helen backed off with Solo. The sight of Sultan rearing up, with the hill dipping away to either side, scared her. He needed room to steady up and calm down. 'Here, Speckle, here, Scruffy!' She slid from the saddle to lead the pony to a safe distance, saw Scruffy come limping towards her.

By this time, Hannah was fighting to get Sultan back under control. Sweat poured from him as he reared and fought back. Down he went and she rocked forward, struggling for balance. The ground beneath her looked hard, dangerous, and a long way to fall.

'Steady, boy!' Once again she tried to rein him in. He was strong and beginning to panic and his stamping hooves crunched off the narrow track and slid over the loose shale. The sound of scree sliding and crashing into rocks frightened them all.

'Here, Scruffy!' Helen held Solo's reins with one hand as she stooped to examine the mongrel's leg. There was a small cut on the ankle. His mouth hung open and his little pink tongue lolled out, as, bewildered and gasping, he let her look.

Then, suddenly, the stamping hooves stopped

thundering on to the loose rocks. Sultan stood and quivered beneath Hannah, his breath rasping, his knees buckling under her weight.

The silence was almost worse than the noise of his protests. What was wrong? Quickly she slid off his back and stepped forward to stroke his cheek and neck. 'There,' she said softly. His whole body shook as if he was freezing cold, yet the sweat lathered him from top to toe.

He looked back at her with a wild, rolling eye. Then, without warning, his legs gave way and he was down, sliding over the edge, helpless. Hannah hung on to the reins, felt herself pulled in his wake as he went crashing down the steep slope.

'Hannah, let go!' Helen cried. She left Solo standing, scrambled down the slope after them. The weight of the horse took Hannah with him as he crashed ten – twenty metres down.

Helen flew after them, struggling to keep her footing. She grabbed at bushes with her free hand, felt the sharp stones slide, saw the dust rise.

'Hannah!' Helen screamed again. 'Let go of the reins! Save yourself. Let Sultan go!'

Three

After what seemed like an age, Sultan crashed against a rock and stopped. Hannah slid into him, tangled in the reins, within range of his flailing hooves. Then this too stopped. All was quiet.

'Are you OK?' By the time Helen and Speckle reached them, Sultan lay still.

Hannah drew breath then crawled free of the unconscious horse. She was shaking and dizzy, feeling sick from the shock. 'We need help!' she cried. Sultan was still breathing, but he couldn't be moved.

Helen looked up the slope to where Solo

stood. 'We're miles from anywhere!'

'It doesn't matter, you'll have to ride Solo to fetch help. We need a vet.' Hannah took charge. 'I'll stay here with Sultan. You go, Helen!'

'Where to?' Helen's only idea was to mount Solo and race along the ridge towards High Peak until she caught up with the leader of the trek. But this could be wasting time, she knew.

'Sally Freeman lives near here,' Hannah said. She crouched by the injured horse and stroked his neck. Taking off her padded riding-jacket, she placed it gently over his heaving sides.

'At High Peak House!' Helen remembered the address of the Doveton vet. Sally was a friend of the family, and her son, Ashley, went to the same school as the twins. 'I'll go there!' Quickly she began to scramble for the top of the ridge. 'I'll take Scruffy. Mrs Freeman can treat the cut on his leg too.'

'Can he walk that far?' Hannah watched her go.

'He doesn't have to; he can sit on Solo.' Gently she picked up the whimpering dog, who waited for her on the ridge, and caught hold of the pony's reins. 'Do you want Speckle to stay here?' she called.

'No. Take him with you.' Hannah gave him the command to leave her side and join Helen. 'He can run ahead and warn Mrs Freeman!' She had already thought it through. Though she was scared and still trembling, her head was clear.

'Are you sure you'll be OK?' Helen was up on Solo with Scruffy resting across the saddle in front of her, looking up at her with his trusting brown eyes. She could just see Hannah ten metres or so down the slope, crouched over Sultan's chestnut form. He lay with his neck stretched up and back, eyes closed, legs folded under him.

Hannah peered back and nodded. 'Be as quick as you can!' she whispered.

Eagerly Solo set off for help. He seemed to know that it was urgent, treading fearlessly along the ridge without looking to left or right until the track dipped and split into two directions; one that followed the bridle-path and the main trekking party, one that sloped across the fellside towards a scattering of houses dotted on the far hill.

Helen steered him on to the lower path. 'This way, Speckle!' She called the Border collie back from the high track. They made their way at a trot over the smoother ground, leaving behind the scree of loose stones that made the ridge so treacherous. 'Please let Mrs Freeman be in!' she said to herself. High Peak House was still a small dot on the far hillside. Time was ticking by, and the picture of Sultan lying unconscious on the ridge pushed her urgently on. 'Please don't let Hannah lose her nerve!' she whispered.

Hannah let her hand rest on Sultan's neck. She'd felt for his pulse and found it just below his cheek. It was faint and uneven, a bad sign, she knew.

'Please let Helen have got there already, and please let Mrs Freeman be at home!' she prayed, crouched over the horse and staring up at the blue sky.

What could she do to help him? His saddle was skewed to one side so she undid the girth strap and slid it out from under him, leaving him free to breathe. Then she unfastened the bridle and eased the headstrap over his ears, slipping the metal bit out of his mouth and pulling the whole thing clear. Checking carefully, she made sure that there were no obvious cuts from the fall. If Sultan had injured himself, it must be internal. She worried about the fact that he was unconscious, another bad sign. 'Please hurry, Helen!' she sighed.

'Go on, Speckle! Go on, Solo!' Helen ordered the dog on ahead and urged the pony into a canter as they reached the lonely road leading to High Peak House. Scruffy lay across the saddle, whimpering as crimson blood oozed from the wound on his foot.

Speckle raced on, ears back, tail flat, galloping along the last stretch of road. He barked to attract attention as he went.

The house was quiet. The sun shone on its greenish slate roof, its pretty white gables and small cottage windows. A pink clematis grew up round the closed front door.

'Oh no!' Helen groaned. There was no answer to Speckle's bark. What would they do if Mrs Freeman wasn't at home?

Speckle barked again. The sound echoed round the empty yard to the side of the house. He jumped a low stone wall and raced across the garden.

'What's he seen?' She spoke aloud, pulling Solo up and dismounting to open the wide gate and lift Scruffy down from the saddle. Speckle had disappeared from view. Then he reappeared, racing up the slope on the far side of the garden, cutting across the hillside to rejoin the road half a mile ahead. He ran like the wind, a black and white speck on the green fields.

Helen studied the road and gasped when she saw what had drawn Speckle away from High Peak House. It was Mrs Freeman's green four-wheel drive, heading up the winding hill towards High Peak. And now Speckle was alongside, head back, obviously barking, though he was too far away to hear. He ran determindly at the car as a sheepdog worries a sheep, darting at it with his head low, in a menacing crouch, herding it into the pen.

'Oh no!' She could hardly bear to look. She held Scruffy close, hooking Solo's reins over the gatepost. Unless Mrs Freeman saw Speckle, there could be a terrible accident.

But the vet did spot him. She stopped the car, got out, bent over to greet Speckle, who jumped up at her, then ran off down the road, begging her to turn round. He did it once, twice, three times, until Sally Freeman understood. She climbed back into the car, reversed it into a gateway and turned in the narrow lane.

Helen drew a deep sigh of relief. 'Good old Speckle!' The vet was driving towards her, following the dog down the road. As soon as she came within view, Helen raised a hand to signal she was there.

'Helen! What's happened to Scruffy?' Sally Freeman stopped the car at the gate and jumped out. She let Ashley out of the passenger side and both came running into the yard.

'I'm so glad Speckle found you!' Her words tumbled out. And she was more relieved than she could say to see the vet; her fair, wavy hair, her silver earrings and bright turquoise jacket. 'Scruffy's cut his foot on a stone.' She delivered the cream-coloured mongrel into safe hands.

'Right. Come inside and we'll see what we can do for him.' She led the way, carrying the dog carefully down the hall into a room at the back where she kept medicines and equipment. 'Luckily I keep some first-aid stuff up here as well as down at the surgery in Doveton.'

'Scruffy's not the only one who's hurt,' Helen rushed on. She described where she'd left Hannah and Sultan as Sally Freeman pulled sterile packets of lint and bandages from a drawer and began to clip the long hair back from the patch of skin surrounding the dog's wound.

Straight away Mrs Freeman changed her tactics. 'Ashley, run and fetch your daddy,' she told her little boy. 'He's having a sleep because he was up all night last night helping a cow to calf at High Hartwell.'

Turning to Helen, she described her new plan. 'We'll leave Scruffy here with Noel. He'll be in good hands. He'll look after Scruffy and see that Solo gets a rest until you can pick him up later. But you and Speckle have to come with me in the car and show me the exact spot where Sultan collapsed.'

Noel Freeman came in just as Sally had finished explaining what they should do. A trained vet himself, he calmly took over Scruffy's treatment. 'Don't worry about a thing,' he assured Helen. 'He looks a tough little customer to me. We'll soon have him strapped up and ready to come home.'

So Helen, Speckle and Sally Freeman were free to race out again to the car and head off up the bridle-path, the way Helen had come down on Solo.

'I'll be back soon,' Helen promised the pony, sorry to leave him behind.

'Come on!' Mrs Freeman had turned the car, ready to go.

Helen jumped in after Speckle, and held on as the car lurched over the rough track. It swayed and rocked into dips, over jutting rocks, climbing the slope to the long, jagged ridge between Doveton Fell and High Peak.

'Tell me what happened.' Mrs Freeman needed the details. 'Did Sultan just collapse without warning?'

'Sort of. He wasn't well. We'd been worried about him since we set off on the trek.' Helen thought back through the morning's events.

'How do you mean, "not well"?' The vet swerved to miss a deep dip in the track.

Helen held on tight. 'Slower than usual. At first we thought he was being awkward, but then Hannah noticed he was sweating.'

'Was he restless?'

She nodded. 'He couldn't breathe very well, then his legs started to shake and he just keeled over.'

'Could be colic,' Sally Freeman said quietly. 'That's when a horse gets a blockage in his gut. It would cause those sorts of symptoms.'

They'd reached the ridge and were driving along the level, between one fellside and the next. Helen recognised a twisted hawthorn bush on the horizon, not far from where Sultan had gone down. She pointed to it and hung on again as the vet increased speed.

'Stop here!' she cried. They couldn't see Hannah and Sultan, but this was the spot. She pointed out the scuffed prints in the soft soil by the bush, then flung open the door to let Speckle jump down.

Out of sight, by the rock where Sultan had landed, Hannah heard the car engine, the squeal of brakes and the crunch of loose stones as it skidded to a halt. How long had Helen been gone? It felt like days, but really could only have been less than two hours. Now she stood and waved them down. 'Sultan's conscious!' she cried. 'He came round a few minutes ago, but he still can't move!'

'OK.' Sally Freeman took in the scene. She gave Helen a rug from the back of the car, grabbed her bag and began to climb down the slope. 'Put that over him to keep him warm,' she told her. She took out a stethoscope and listened to Sultan's heart and lungs. 'Not colic,' she said with a frown.

Helen and Hannah covered him with the rug. He lay looking up at them, seeming to know why they were there. All his pride and awkwardness were gone. Now he was just a sick animal badly in need of help.

'What's this horse been eating lately?' the vet asked as she looked into his mouth. There was a trickle of saliva dribbling on to the rock where he lay.

Hannah shook her head. 'Just normal, I think. He's out in the paddock most of the time, so I suppose he eats mainly fresh grass.'

Sally Freeman shook her head and listened again with her stethoscope. 'You say he lost condition. How long ago?'

'Not long. Just yesterday.' Helen tried to remember. She watched the vet draw down Sultan's bottom eyelid and peer into the eye.

'Did he stagger before he fell?'

Hannah nodded. 'A bit.' His legs had gone weak and shaky, she remembered, then he'd staggered sideways. 'What is it? What's wrong with him?'

Mrs Freeman stood up, deep lines creasing her forehead. 'If I'm not mistaken, I think this fellow's eaten something he shouldn't have.'

'Like what?' Hannah looked at Helen. What could the vet mean?

'Like he's been licking creosote from a fence, or nibbling at a privet hedge. Or he could have been eating something like foxglove or ragwort in the grass at the side of the road.' She checked his pulse and nodded. 'In fact, I'm fairly sure I know the problem now.' Helen dropped her gaze and stared at the ground as Mrs Freemen pronounced the verdict. 'I'm afraid Sultan's been poisoned, and it could be very serious indeed.'

Four

Sally Freeman took out her mobile phone and rang Fred Hunt, the farmer at nearby High Hartwell Farm. She asked him to drive up to the ridge with a trailer.

'Quick as you can, Fred. We've got a horse from the Three Peaks trek that's collapsed with suspected food poisoning, and it's not looking too good. I've checked for broken bones and I think we're OK there, but we need transport to get him home to Doveton Manor double quick.' She got her message across, then turned back to Sultan and the twins.

'OK, Hannah, I want you to stay by his head while I take his temperature and check for any injuries he might have sustained in the fall. Talk to him, try to keep him calm.'

Since he'd come round, the horse had tried time and again to lift his head and roll on to his knees so that he could stand up. But he was too weak, and he would sink back exhausted after a short struggle. Seeing him helpless made Hannah want to cry out. But she knew she must do as the vet asked without giving way. So she knelt on the stony ground and whispered, 'There, Sultan, lie still. You'll soon feel better, and a trailer is on its way to take you home!'

'Come on, Helen, don't just stand there!' Sally had reached for her bag and taken out a syringe. 'We're going to give him a tetanus jab and clean up this cut on his knee while we're waiting for Fred.'

Helen stared as if she hadn't heard. She felt the blood drain from her face and shook her head as she looked away.

'What's wrong?' Hannah still stroked Sultan's neck. She could feel his pulse racing, heard Mrs

Freeman mutter that his temperature was very low. 'Helen!'

'Nothing. It doesn't matter.' A thousand thoughts whirled inside her head. They seemed to stop her from rushing in to help. All she could do was stand and stare as the vet cleaned Sultan's leg wound, dried it and dusted it with a white powder. Speckle, too, seemed dazed and puzzled. He sat beside Helen, watching quietly, wondering why Sultan couldn't get on to his feet.

'What now?' Hannah asked. Sultan was looking at her quietly, his gaze fixed on her face.

Sally Freeman came and examined his mouth. 'Well, the slobbering seems to be slightly better.' Gently she eased the horse's jaws open. 'I can't see any burns or blisters, so it's unlikely to be creosote that's poisoned him.'

'Is that good?'

'Not necessarily. We could treat him with Epsom salts if it was creosote that was the problem. With some other forms of poisoning, there's no known treatment, I'm afraid.'

'No known treatment?' For the first time since they'd arrived, Helen spoke.

Mrs Freeman shone a slim torch into the patient's eyes. 'Not if he's eaten something like privet or foxglove.'

Helen felt another jolt of fear. 'You mean he would die?'

'Yes, and pretty quickly. With foxglove poisoning it would only be a matter of hours.'

Helen hung her head, turned away and muttered, 'It can't be that.'

'What?' Hannah couldn't hear.

'Nothing.'

'I don't think it's foxglove.' The vet seemed to echo Helen's thoughts. 'I can tell from his eyes that he's suffering from jaundice, which means liver damage, and I'm beginning to suspect it must be ragwort that's the culprit.' She was brisk as she stood up and tidied things back into her bag. 'Did you hear a car?' she asked.

They listened and waited. An engine chugged up the hill from Doveton Fell, still hidden from view. They recognised the rattle of the Land Rover engine. In a few minutes Fred Hunt would be there.

'It's time to try and get Sultan on to his feet,'

Mrs Freeman decided. She asked Hannah to slip the horse's bridle back on. 'With a bit of encouragement, we should be able to get him into the trailer,' she assured them. 'And then at least we can get him back to the comfort of his own stable.'

So they coaxed Sultan and praised him when he gathered enough strength to lift himself on to his knees.

'Good boy,' Hannah whispered, holding the bridle and encouraging him as the farmer's Land Rover came into view on top of the ridge. While Sally Freeman ran to speak to Fred, Speckle crept closer, wagging his tail as if this too would help. But Helen stood rooted to the spot, her face pale, her dark eyes staring.

Patiently Hannah urged Sultan to stand. 'Just for a little while,' she pleaded. She could hear the farmer backing the trailer into position and lowering the ramp. 'Come on, Sultan, you can do it!'

'Easy does it!' Fred Hunt's deep voice warned. He took in the situation at a glance. A lifetime of farming told him how serious it was. But he didn't flap or fuss, just took the bridle from Hannah and put a broad hand firmly on Sultan's flank. 'Up!' he said, and Sultan responded, raising himself on shaky legs, tottering as he stood.

'Just a few steps!' Hannah breathed. She went to stand by Helen, watching the horse sway and stagger. Sally Freeman slung the rug over his back and urged him on from behind as Fred Hunt led him steadily up the metal ramp and into the straw-lined trailer.

'Jump in my car, girls!' Mrs Freeman snapped into action as soon as the horse was safely in the trailer.

Helen and Hannah ordered Speckle into the back of the vet's car and followed him.

Mr Hunt made sure that Sultan, weak as he was, wouldn't stagger and crash into the sides of the box as he drove down the fell. Then he bolted the door into place and took his seat behind the wheel. 'Ready?' he cried.

'We'll follow you!' Mrs Freeman shouted back. She put the car in gear and revved the engine, then she leaned out of the window again. 'Shall I ring Geoffrey Saunders and warn him?'

Hannah frowned and looked at Helen's pale, blank face. This was one of the worst parts; having to face up to Mr and Mrs Saunders when they got back to the Manor.

'No need!' The old farmer eased the Land Rover and trailer along the ridge, away from the accident spot. 'I did that myself before I set off from High Hartwell. Thought he should know what to expect.'

'What did he say?' Sally Freeman cried.

Helen closed her eyes, Hannah stared ahead at Sultan's head and neck, just visible above the trailer door. He swayed and staggered as they turned on to a track and began the descent.

'He's not pleased.' Fred's gruff voice carried back on the wind. 'Not pleased at all!'

'Oh, what will Laura say?' Val Saunders held both hands to her mouth as the vet and Fred Hunt led Sultan, trembling and shaking under the heavy rug, out of the trailer and into the stables at Doveton Manor. 'It will break her heart when we tell her!'

Sally Freeman had confirmed Fred's news the

moment the Saunders rushed out to meet them. 'He's very sick,' she repeated. 'I'll do everything I can, but you mustn't hold out any false hopes. A case like this most often proves fatal.'

'Forget about Laura.' Geoffrey Saunders brushed his wife to one side as he strode over to Helen and Hannah. 'Let's get to the bottom of this, shall we? Exactly what's been going on?'

'We're sorry,' Hannah gasped. Mr Saunders towered over them, his dark eyebrows knitted together, glaring at them as if it must be their fault that Sultan was dangerously ill. 'I knew he wasn't well right from the start but I didn't realise how bad it was.' Tears filled Hannah's eyes, then slid down her cheeks.

Beyond Mr Saunders, Sultan had disappeared into his stable. The white door hung open, they could hear him stagger and collapse against the side of the wooden stall before he crashed to the ground. Mrs Freeman's voice gave worried instructions, Fred Hunt grunted his replies.

'Food poisoning!' Mr Saunders repeated the diagnosis. 'How? When? Where? There are no poisonous substances round here!'

49

Mrs Saunders came and laid a hand on his arm. 'Never mind that now. What matters is Sultan. If he's as ill as we think, he'll need lots of care.' She tried to persuade her husband not to be hard on the twins.

But he was looking for someone to blame. 'I want some answers. We send a perfectly fit horse out on a trek that animals half his size and twice his age can easily manage. And he comes back at death's door!' The more he talked, the more worked-up he grew. 'Well?'

Hannah shook her head. She couldn't find any words to explain what had happened.

He turned to Helen. 'What did you let him eat?' he demanded.

'Nothing!' Hannah broke in. 'I was riding him, and he didn't eat anything.'

'You must have.' Mr Saunders hurried them all across the yard towards Sultan's paddock. He spread his arms wide. 'You take a good look,' he insisted. 'You can go over every inch of this pasture, and I'll guarantee it's clean. No foxgloves, no vetch, no ragwort. I'll bet my life you won't find a single shoot of any poisonous plant in there!'

'Geoffrey!' Mrs Saunders protested mildly. She could see that Hannah was still in tears.

'No. There has to be some explanation for this.' He turned to Helen. 'You haven't said much so far. I take it you know more than you're saying?'

'Geoffrey, the twins aren't necessarily to blame!'

Helen looked up at her tall inquisitor. Her knees trembled, her mouth was dry.

Geoffrey Saunders frowned back at her. He folded his arms and waited. 'Sultan's dying,' he insisted. 'He's an expensive thoroughbred, and what's more, he means the world to Laura. I think I deserve an explanation.'

Silence. The breeze rustled through the grass and the new leaves in the beech trees lining the paddock fence. Back in the stables, Sultan gave a faint whinny.

'It must have been me,' Helen admitted at last, her voice a cracked whisper. 'Yesterday. I let him eat from the hedge by the cricket pitch.' She turned to Hannah with a sob. 'I didn't know – but it was me. I poisoned him!'

Five

'To think when we first came to Home Farm, I used to be scared of Fred Hunt!' Mary Moore admitted.

It was late in the afternoon of the disastrous Three Peaks trek. Thanks to the farmer, everyone was safely home, including Solo. Fred Hunt had just fetched him in the trailer from High Peak House where he'd called to collect the injured Scruffy for the Moores.

Now he was waving from his Land Rover, telling the twins not to feel too bad about poor old Sultan, heading back to his wife, Hilda, and their herd of Friesian cows in time for evening milking.

'No, he's got a heart of pure gold,' David Moore insisted. He stood with an arm round Helen's shoulder, watching the farmer drive off. 'And he's right. Even if you did let Sultan nibble at something he shouldn't have, you couldn't have been expected to know. It's just one of those things.'

Helen stood, miserable and guilty, until Scruffy came limping over to her with his bandaged foot, then she stopped to pick him up. She buried her face in his soft cream fur.

'I'll see to Solo,' Hannah said quietly. She was eager to keep busy, leading him to the barn where they kept his grooming kit. He stood patiently as she took off his saddle and bridle, hung them up, then brushed him down, working from head to tail. Then she covered him with his night rug before leading him out again into the field behind the farm.

For a few minutes after she'd put him out to grass, she sat on the wall watching him, until she grew cold in the evening shadows. She shivered and jumped to the ground, ran across the farmyard, past the hens pecking and scratching in the dust, past Speckle and Scruffy sitting side by side on the doorstep.

'Where's Helen?' she asked her dad, who was busy making supper.

'Upstairs.' He glanced up. 'See if you can cheer her up,' he suggested. 'Your mum and I have both failed. We're worried about her.'

So Hannah kicked off her boots and went up to their room. She found Helen lying on her bed, staring up at the sloping white ceiling.

'Supper's nearly ready,' she said casually, pretending nothing was wrong. She began to change out of her riding things into a clean T-shirt and jeans.

'Not hungry,' came the quiet reply.

Now Hannah was worried too. 'You're *never* not hungry!' she teased.

'Leave me alone,' Helen murmured. 'I'm not in the mood.' She turned on to her side and faced the wall. 'Honest, Hannah, I don't want to talk.'

Hannah sat on the edge of her bed. 'I'm supposed to be cheering you up,' she confessed with a sigh.

'You can't. Nobody can.' It hadn't needed Mr

Saunders to point his finger and practically accuse her of killing Laura's horse. She already had a cold and certain feeling that she was to blame. She'd been careless, she should have known better. Time after time she accused herself, going back in her own mind to the moment the day before when she'd let Sultan drop his head and graze the lethal plants.

'Helen-Hannah, phone!' Mary Moore called from downstairs.

Helen shot upright on the bed. 'I bet that's Laura! She'll be ringing to ask us how Sultan managed the Three Peaks.'

Hannah nodded. 'I'll go.'

'What will you tell her?'

'The truth, I expect.' She went down slowly, trying to think of a way to soften the news, dreading the moment when she had to pick up the phone.

But when she got there, the handset was back on its hook. Her mum hovered nearby with a small frown on her normally cheerful face.

'Was that Laura?' Hannah asked.

'No; it was her mum ringing from Doveton

Manor. She changed her mind about speaking to you and asked me to pass on a message instead.'

'What did she say?' Hannah hadn't expected to hear from the Saunders after they'd left the Manor in disgrace. 'Sultan isn't dead, is he?'

'No.' Mary shrugged. 'It was a bit peculiar, really. She asked me to ask you and Helen not to mention anything about Sultan's illness to Laura when she rings you.'

'How can we not tell her?' Laura would want to know every tiny detail about the trek; how long they'd taken to finish, whether or not Sultan had behaved.

'I know. And that's not all. Valerie asked me to ask you to go and see her at the Manor tomorrow morning. Geoffrey will be out playing golf, so she says there's no need to be scared. She's not angry with you.'

'Anything else?' Hannah was still puzzled.

'Yes. She said she'd already spoken to Laura. That's what she wants to see you about.'

'Do you think we should go?'

'I don't know. How do you feel?'

'Terrible. And Helen feels even worse. And if

we do go tomorrow, we'll probably see Sultan . . .'

'Don't you want to?' Her mum waited for her to make up her mind.

'I do and I don't. I can't stop thinking about him all the time, wondering if he's getting worse . . .' She paced up and down the kitchen, frowning at the floor.

'For what it's worth, Valerie said he seemed to be holding his own at the moment.'

Hannah glanced up. Maybe Sultan wasn't quite so ill as Sally Freeman had first thought. 'OK,' she agreed. 'I don't think Helen will come, but I'll go anyway!'

'Sultan's being the ideal patient, bless him!' Valerie Saunders told Sally Freeman.

'He certainly seems to be doing as he's told!' The vet had called at the same time as Hannah. They'd arrived at the stone gates together, and Mrs Freeman had given her a lift up the long drive.

So far there had been no chance for Laura's mother to take Hannah to one side and tell her why she'd asked her to visit. Instead, Mrs Freeman enlisted her help.

'I'm taking blood samples to test Sultan for jaundice,' she explained. Hannah saw the horse quiver as the needle went in. 'After this, I want to give him a dose of Epsom salts in warm water. You hold his head while I push this tube down his throat into his stomach.'

'What's it for?' Hannah did as she was asked. Poor Sultan didn't seem to have the strength to object to the nasty plastic tube. So she stroked him and kept him as calm as possible while the vet did her work.

'It acts as an antidote to some poisons. I gave him one dose yesterday, and it's just possible that it's had some effect. Of course, we can't be sure because we don't know exactly what it was that Sultan ate.'

'What I don't understand is how something as small as one shoot of a plant can do this to a horse.' After all, Sultan had seemed so big and strong.

'It only takes a tiny amount. I've known a couple of mouthfuls of foxglove finish a horse off within hours!'

Hannah shuddered and frowned. 'Good boy!'

she told Sultan as Mrs Freeman took the tube out and packed away her things.

'I'll call back later today,' the vet promised. 'We should have some results through from the lab by then.' She patted Sultan's neck as she left Hannah and Mrs Saunders to themselves.

'Thank you for coming.' Laura's mother watched from the stable door as Hannah settled Sultan back into his bed of straw. 'And I'm sorry Geoffrey was so cross with Helen. It was partly the shock; he's very fond of Sultan. We all are.'

Hannah stroked the horse's velvety brown muzzle and stepped back from the quiet stall. 'Mum said you'd told Laura the bad news.'

'Ah! That's what I want to talk to you about.' Mrs Saunders took Hannah out into the yard. She spoke quickly and earnestly. 'It's true I've spoken to Laura since this happened. I rang her at school. But Geoffrey and I had already decided not to tell her about Sultan's illness.'

'Not tell her?' Hannah frowned. Had she heard this right?

'Yes. We know how she would worry if she knew Sultan was ill. And she has exams in a few weeks' time. We felt it would upset her too much.' Mrs Saunders' voice faded, and she sighed. 'It was Geoffrey's idea, really. He absolutely insisted that Laura didn't find out!'

Hannah nodded. 'And you want Helen and me to keep quiet too?' Now she understood why she'd been called to the Manor.

Valerie Saunders pushed a stray lock of blonde hair behind her ear and looked away. 'Would you promise not to say a word until after Laura has finished her exams?'

'You mean, lie to her?'

'Not lie, exactly. Just avoid the subject.'

'How can we? She always rings and asks us how Sultan's been behaving, where we've been riding him, how he's looking. We can't just refuse to answer!' Hannah stared. 'It's not possible!'

'Well, couldn't you say he's fine, or pretend you haven't been to see him lately?' Mrs Saunders' pale, smooth face had blushed deep red.

'She'd ask why not!' Hannah knew Laura too well. 'She wouldn't let us fob her off!'

'Then yes, lie!' Biting her lip, Laura's mother looked straight at Hannah. 'Imagine how you'd feel if Sultan was your horse and you were away at school, knowing he was seriously ill!' She waited for this to sink in. When she saw Hannah give a faint nod, she went on. 'So you promise not to tell? . . . For Laura's sake!'

'You look as if you've got a lot on your mind,' Luke Martin said to Hannah.

She passed the shop as she cycled back through the village. Luke stood at the door watching the world go by. He loved to talk to anyone who had the time.

'Where's Helen?' he asked. Luke was used to seeing the twins go everywhere together.

'At home.' She stopped and leaned her bike against the kerb, looking up at the white doves fluttering on the roof. They cooed gently and spread their fan-shaped tails.

'Still feeling bad about yesterday?' The whole village had heard about poor Sultan. Luke knew how the twins must feel.

Hannah nodded. 'She wouldn't even eat breakfast.'

Luke tutted and rubbed his beard. 'Not eating!'

'I know. It's that bad.' She sat on the bench outside the shop, flopping back and closing her eyes. 'Anyone would think she'd picked those plants and deliberately stuffed them into Sultan's mouth!' She'd left Helen at home, wandering from room to room, not even bothering to get dressed or pay any attention to Scruffy, who was limping after her, faithful little dog that he was.

'Whereas, in fact, it was a complete fluke.' Luke sat beside her. He spoke slowly, never hurried, never in a bad mood. The only thing he ever grew excited about was the local cricket team and the matches they played on the pitch down the road. He cared for that cricket field more than anything, and he wasn't ashamed to admit it.

This fact struck Hannah as she sat with him now. 'Luke . . .' She hesitated. 'You know where Sultan is supposed to have eaten this poisonous plant that's making him so ill?'

'No. Where?'

'Well, Helen says it was along the grass verge by your cricket pitch!'

The words 'cricket pitch' made Luke jump to his feet. 'Where?' he demanded.

'By the hedge. That's where Sultan stopped to nibble.'

'And they're saying he ate these poisonous weeds by my hedge!' Luke frowned, as if he couldn't believe his ears. 'What kind of weeds, for a start?'

Hannah also got up. 'Maybe foxgloves. And what was the other one? Ragwort!'

'Foxgloves! Ragwort! Never!' He strode off down the street to prove it. 'A weed like ragwort wouldn't so much as dare show its face anywhere near my pitch!' he declared, frightening Mr Winter's dog, who snuffled as usual at the garden gate. People stared as Luke broke into a trot.

'Luke, wait!' Hannah ran after him.

'No, come and look.' He reached the gate, then the neat, clipped hawthorn hedge that ran the length of the pitch. Beneath it was a tidy, well-mown strip of grass. 'Not a weed in sight!' he declared proudly.

Hannah paused for breath. 'What would fox-gloves look like?' She wanted to make sure that Luke was right.

'Big, broad leaves, quite furry. No flowers yet. It's too early in the year. But you can spot the leaves easy as anything. Likewise with ragwort. The leaves are feathery and curly. But look, can you see even a daisy poking its head through? No, you bet your life you can't!'

Hannah studied the grass verge. It was smooth and perfect. If this was where Sultan had stooped to graze, there wasn't a weed or wild flower to be found. 'You're right!' she gasped.

'Of course I'm right.' Luke knew every blade of grass.

'But you know what this means?' Hannah grasped at the discovery.

Luke nodded. He smiled and called after her as she raced back to the shop for her bike, 'This lets Helen off the hook!'

Hannah was already pedalling furiously for home. 'Helen didn't poison Sultan!' she cried to anyone who would listen. 'It can't be true! It's not her fault after all!'

Six

'I only wish it made a difference to Sultan,' Helen sighed. Yes, she was pleased that Hannah had proved it wasn't her fault. Yes, it meant a lot to her that she'd come down to Doveton Manor and that Mr Saunders had actually said sorry.

'I admit I was rather hasty in blaming you,' he'd said to Helen when he came home from golf. 'And I've been too busy lately to pay proper attention to Sultan. That's why he's been a bit difficult; I haven't given him enough time. It lets a horse develop bad habits, through boredom as much as anything.'

They'd begun to wonder all over again where the sick horse could possibly have eaten the poisonous plant.

Helen and Hannah had left Mr and Mrs Saunders to talk to the vet about the new situation. Now they stood inside the stable, stroking Sultan who lay feebly in the straw, hardly able to raise his head. Helen patted his velvety muzzle and sighed again.

'He looks so sad,' Hannah whispered. 'Do you think he knows what's happening to him?'

'He must know he's sick. I don't suppose he knows why.'

Sultan nuzzled back at the palm of her hand, his long black mane drooping over the white star on his forehead, his usually gleaming coat dull and damp.

Hannah took a stable rubber from the bench and began to gently rub his neck and sides. 'I don't think even I know why!' she murmured.

'That's because we don't know enough about horse illnesses.' Helen felt helpless because of it.

'But Mrs Freeman does.' Hannah could hear the grown-ups talking about the patient in low, serious voices. The vet had come back, as promised, to check on the horse, and it sounded as if she was giving the Saunders more bad news.

'. . . Blood test results . . . not good . . . definite jaundice and damage to the liver . . .' Sally Freeman's voice drifted in through the stable door.

Hannah and Helen crouched beside Sultan and strained to hear.

'Can't anything be done?' Mr Saunders wanted to know.

'We don't care what it would cost to get Sultan better.' Mrs Saunders sounded desperate. 'Isn't there some kind of treatment that might work?'

There was a long pause. 'You can't reverse liver damage caused by certain forms of poisoning,' Sally Freeman explained. 'And Sultan hasn't responded to the antidotes.'

Another silence followed, filled by the horse's soft breathing. Hannah stared at Helen, preparing for the worst.

'Try something else!' Mrs Saunders pleaded.

'I'm afraid there's no further treatment. Just careful nursing to keep the patient comfortable.'

The vet's voice was full of regret as she gave her verdict.

'How long has he got?' Mr Saunders asked.

'I can't say for sure. He'll probably go downhill slowly but surely. In Sultan's case, it could be several weeks before he dies.'

'Try not to take it too hard,' David Moore told the twins. He had found them that Sunday evening, huddled inside the barn at Home Farm, with tearstained faces. They'd come home from Doveton Manor in a daze. They hadn't even been able to face going into the house.

But Speckle had seen them creep into the empty barn and come scratching at the door. After a few minutes, Mr Moore had come out to investigate.

Hannah had sobbed out the latest news about Sultan, so he sat on a bale of straw between them, one arm round each of their shoulders.

'That's what happens when you keep animals; they sometimes get sick and die. It's life, I'm afraid.'

Helen's insides hurt from crying. 'Sultan isn't

going to get better!' Nothing else mattered; not Speckle pushing his nose into her lap, nor Scruffy limping into the barn and staring up at her with his huge brown eyes.

'No, we know he's not.' Her dad gave her a squeeze. 'It feels very bad right now. And he's not even your horse. Just imagine how Laura must be feeling.'

The name Laura lifted Hannah out of her daze. 'She doesn't know,' she whispered, sniffing and doing her best to stop crying.

'Why not? Hasn't anyone telephoned her?'

'Yes. Her mum rang yesterday, but she decided not to say anything. And we're not allowed to tell her either.'

David Moore frowned. 'That could be a bit hard.'

'I won't be able to talk to her,' Helen decided. 'I know my voice would sound funny. She'd guess something was wrong.'

'Me too.' Hannah sniffed again. She took Scruffy on to her knee.

'What's the idea?' Their easy-going father sounded cross. 'I suppose the Saunders think they're protecting Laura, but she'll have to find out in the end. If Sultan's as sick as you say he is—'

'He is!' Helen insisted.

'Well, then, poor Laura's going to get even more of a shock if the horse dies without her even knowing that he's ill. Surely it would be better to prepare her!'

'She's got exams.' Hannah gave the reason. 'They don't want to upset her right now.'

'Hmm.' David Moore stood up and thoughtfully picked pieces of straw from his sweater. 'I don't think it's right to involve you two in the deceit,' he pointed out. 'Let me talk to your mum about it when she gets back from the cafe.'

'Difficult!' Mary Moore agreed. She'd come home after a busy day serving daytrippers in Nesfield with pots of tea, scones and home-made cakes. Now the whole family sat together round the big kitchen table. 'This food poisoning business; you don't think it'd be worthwhile getting a second opinion?'

'It seems Sally's pretty sure,' David Moore pointed out. The vet was their friend and they knew she was good at her job.

'Even though they haven't found any evidence of where the plants could be growing?' Mary had listened, taken in everything that the twins had told her as soon as she'd stepped through the door.

'You mean she might not be right?' Helen seized on this. It dawned on her that even a good vet could sometimes get things wrong.

'Sultan might not be dying?' Hannah hardly dared to hope. 'There could be a cure?' It was like someone lighting a flame in a dark cave; new hope that Sultan could live after all.

'No.' Their dad laid both palms flat on the table. 'We have to accept it. If Sally says Sultan has been poisoned, that's that, I'm afraid. I don't see how we could question her opinion.'

He shook his head, then changed the subject. 'It makes me wish you two had never got involved with looking after Sultan in the first place.'

'Oh no!' Helen cried. 'We don't wish that. He's brilliant to ride when he's behaving himself . . . *was* brilliant . . .' She faltered, sniffed and turned away.

'And we still want to go to the Manor to help nurse him,' Hannah insisted. 'Even if . . . even though we know he's not going to get better . . .' Her voice faded too and she looked down.

'Do you want me or your dad to take the phone calls from Laura?' their mum suggested. 'That way you wouldn't have to talk to her.'

Hannah shook her head. 'She'd still know something was wrong.'

'Yes; she'd wonder why we didn't want to chat about how great Sultan's been, what he's been up to and everything.' Helen stared at the plate of untouched chocolate cake that her mum had brought home. She began to dread the sound of the phone ringing; looked at the clock and then realised that Sunday evening was often a time when Laura got in touch.

'She'll ask about Three Peaks,' Hannah sighed. 'I bet anything she'll ring tonight to talk about that!'

'Her mum can't put her off for ever,' Helen agreed.

Ring-ring! *Ring-ring*!' The phone made them jump out of their seats.

'Oh no!' Helen covered her ears. 'It's Laura; I know it is!'

'You answer it!' Hannah cried at Helen. She wanted to run away, far from the sound of the phone as it drilled into her head.

'I'll go,' Mary Moore said calmly. 'I think I can manage not to give anything away, if that's what Valerie thinks is best.'

'No – I will!' In an instant Helen changed her mind.

'We both will!' Hannah decided it was something they had to do themselves. They'd promised Mrs Saunders, and now she wanted to stick to her word.

Ring-ring! Out in the hall, the phone demanded to be picked up.

'Well, someone had better answer it.' David Moore was making his way out of the kitchen.

But Helen and Hannah scooted past. Helen reached the phone first and picked it up, trying to keep the shakes out of her voice while she learned who it was. 'Hello?'

'Hi, Hannah?'

'No, it's Helen.' She recognised the bubbly, friendly voice straight away. 'It's Laura!' she whispered to Hannah, her hand across the phone.

'Hi, Helen. Sorry I couldn't ring yesterday. We had a school netball match. I sneaked off and spoke to Mummy for literally one minute. She said Three Peaks went fine.'

'Yes. There were loads of people.' Helen swallowed hard.

'What was the weather like? Did it rain? It did here. I couldn't help thinking of poor Sultan getting wet!'

'No, it was fine.'

'How was he? I bet he wasn't keen on trekking up High Peak, was he?'

'Not very.' Helen guarded her answers carefully.

'Come on, Helen, tell me how he got on! I bet he really hated the uphill bits, didn't he?' Laura laughed edgily, waiting for the details.

'He was a bit slow.'

'Was he sulking?' She knew her own horse well. 'I can just picture him hanging back until the crowd had gone on ahead. Typical Sultan!'

'Yes!' Helen bit her lip as her voice wobbled.

'What's wrong? You sound as if you've got a cold.'

'No, I'm OK. Here's Hannah,' she said quickly and jerkily, dropping the phone into Hannah's hand as if it was hot.

'Hi, Hannah. What's up with Helen?'

'Nothing. She thought she was going to sneeze.' Hannah came out with the first thing she could think of. But the lie made her blush deep red as she fumbled with the phone.

'She says Sultan didn't enjoy himself much on the trek.' Doubt was creeping into Laura's voice.

The fizz had gone, she sounded anxious. 'Who was riding him?'

'I was. He was fine, don't worry.'

'Why should I worry?'

'No reason.' Hannah could have kicked herself for not sounding more cheerful.

'He didn't fall, did he?' By now Laura was sure something was wrong. 'He didn't cut his knees?'

'No!'

'He did, didn't he? He fell on one of those horrible screes.'

'No!' Hannah could only squeeze out the denial as a kind of yelp. If only they'd let their mum or dad deal with the phone call.

'I don't believe you. Listen, Hannah, don't lie to me. Something bad has happened, hasn't it? Something terrible!' Panic set in, questions began to pour out. 'If it's not his knees, what is it? Did he fall and break his neck? Is that what happened? That's it! He fell and hurt himself so badly you had to call the vet. Hannah, tell me; did Sultan have to be put down?'

'No!' She croaked an answer. 'He's at home in his stable. He's alive.'

'But he's not OK, is he?' Laura pleaded to know.

'I'm not supposed to say anything!' She clung to the phone until her knuckles turned white.

'Hannah, you can't do this to me! You've got to tell me! . . . Are you still there? Hannah!'

She closed her eyes and let the phone fall, heard Helen pick it up again.

'We can't tell you the truth, Laura. We've been ordered not to. You'd better ring your mum and dad.' It was no use pretending any more.

'Why? What's happened? He is dead, isn't he?'

'No. Ring home,' Helen insisted. 'Get them to tell you.' She waited for Laura to agree.

But there was silence on the other end of the phone.

'Laura? Are you there? Laura, you've got to speak to your mum and dad, please!'

The phone crackled. There was a sudden click and the line went dead.

Seven

'You did the right thing.'

Their dad's words still rang in Hannah and Helen's ears as they lay in bed that night. It was the last thing he said before they kissed him goodnight. He gave them a comforting hug and told them to sleep well.

'Easier said than done,' Helen sighed. Sleep was a million miles away as she stared out of the window and listened to the wind in the tall horse chestnut tree by the farmyard gate.

Hannah squirmed and tossed from side to side under her warm duvet. 'What will Laura do now?'

she whispered into the darkness.

'It's not your problem, girls!' Mary Moore overheard the question as she looked in on them. She was on her way to bed. 'Your dad was right; you did the only thing you could in the circumstances. Now forget about it and get some sleep.'

The leaves in the tree rustled, clouds slid across a crecent moon in the black sky.

'Do you think she rang home?' Helen murmured. The alarm clock by her bed read twelve o'clock, midnight.

'I wonder if they told her the truth.' Hannah stared at the ceiling.

'She probably hung up on us and dialled her mum to find out.'

'They'd have to tell her if she asked them straight out what was wrong with Sultan.'

'Mr and Mrs Saunders will be really mad with us.'

'Even they couldn't tell her an out and out lie!' Hannah imagined that Laura must know the whole story by now.

'They'll say it's our fault if Laura fails her exams.'

Helen didn't know how they'd ever be able to face the Saunders again.

'Girls, for the last time, give it a rest!' David Moore came padding along the corridor in bare feet and pyjamas. He stuck his tousled head round their door. 'First thing in the morning, before you go to school, I'll ring the Manor to find out what's going on. In the meantime, for all our sakes, go to sleep!'

Hannah and Helen appeared next morning pale-faced, with dark rings under their eyes.

'Eat!' Mary Moore ordered before she set off for work. She pushed a plate of fresh toast and jam towards them. 'Drink! You can't go to school without a proper breakfast.'

Hannah took a gulp of orange juice. 'I'm not hungry, Mum.'

'Me neither.' Helen stood at the window, staring across the yard and up the lane. 'Dad, have you rung Doveton Manor?'

'Not yet. It's only seven-thirty. They might not be up.' He was the only one tucking into the toast, washed down with piping hot tea.

Mary Moore came to water her plants on the kitchen windowsill. As she peered out, she heard a car engine coming down the quiet lane. 'Who can this be at this time?' she wondered.

'It's Mrs Freeman.' Helen recognised the Land Rover. It stopped at their gate and the vet got out.

'I wonder what it's about.' David Moore went to meet her.

'Sultan!' Hannah whispered.

Helen nodded. What else would bring Sally Freeman over Hardstone Pass, the back way into town?

'Don't look so worried,' Mrs Freeman told them as she came in, her fair hair held back by a bright blue scarf. She was breezy and cheerful. 'I was just telling your dad; Noel and I have been having a talk about Sultan's case. I told him it was still a bit of a mystery. For instance, we don't know where the horse picked up the poison. Noel thought we should pay another visit to Doveton Manor and check the paddock.'

'We?' Helen frowned and took a step back.

'You mean you, me and Helen?' Hannah asked.

'If you want to. After all, you two have been involved since the beginning. I rang Val Saunders before I left home to check that it would be OK.'

'What did she say?' Hannah was sure that Laura's mother wouldn't want them anywhere near.

'She said "Fine".'

'She didn't mention anything about Laura?' Helen checked.

'Not a word. She said she didn't mind if we called early, then you and Hannah could look in on Sultan and you'd still get to school on time.'

Still surprised, Helen and Hannah found it hard to resist the idea of visiting Sultan.

'Do you want to?' their dad asked.

They both nodded. Before they had time to think, they'd packed their schoolbags and were on their way with the vet, down the lane into the village, and through the gates of Doveton Manor.

'Sometimes it helps to have a new point of view,' Sally Freeman explained as they drew up to the grand house. 'For instance, Noel thought that we shouldn't just accept Mr Saunders' word that Sultan's paddock was free of poisonous weeds. We should check for ourselves. And of course it's still important to find out exactly what it is that Sultan has eaten.'

'It's like putting clues together,' Hannah agreed. She couldn't help being excited as she climbed down from the car.

'Like being a detective!' Helen said.

'Exactly.' Sally Freeman led the way into the paddock without first calling at the house. 'It's OK, they're expecting us,' she reassured Helen and Hannah. 'I told them we'd just get on by ourselves.'

'What are we looking for?' Hannah stepped into the lush green field.

'Good question.' The vet picked stalks of grass to show them. 'Some weeds are OK for horses to eat. Like dandelion, for instance. And this is rye grass, that's OK. So is cock's-foot, ribgrass and sainfoin.' She showed them several shapes and sizes of grass. 'These are all good grazing.'

Helen went over to the fence where the grass grew longer. She stooped to pick a clump of clover leaves. 'What about this?'

'That's OK too. It's a rich food, so too much can cause problems. But that isn't what's made

Sultan so ill.' Mrs Freeman went on searching. 'No; what we're looking for is nasty ragwort.' She stopped suddenly and peered at a pile of Sultan's droppings. 'At least, I think that's what we're looking for!'

'What's wrong?' Hannah asked. Mrs Freeman stood with her head to one side, deep in thought.

'Why didn't I think of that?' she exclaimed. 'Ragwort, foxglove! Foxglove, ragwort! That's all I had in my head. Nothing so simple as this!'

'So simple as what?' Helen and Hannah ran to join her. All they could see was a pile of old horse droppings.

But Mrs Freeman took a plastic bag from her pocket and scooped some up. 'Roundworm,' she said quietly. She looked back at the house, braced herself and began to walk towards it. 'Come on, girls. Let's go and talk to Mr Saunders about when he last dosed Sultan against good old common-or-garden roundworm!'

'Well, no, I have to admit I haven't had time this spring.' The busy owner of Doveton Manor confessed that he hadn't given Sultan the protection he needed. 'You mean to say he might have picked it up from the paddock?'

'By the look of these droppings, yes.' Sally Freeman had broken the news quietly. 'There's definite evidence of roundworms in Sultan's gut, which he's passed on to the pasture. I'll send them off to the lab to be checked, but at the moment that's definitely what it looks like.'

Geoffrey Saunders looked uncomfortable. He tutted and paced up and down the stable yard. 'I kept meaning to do it, but I never found the time,' he muttered. He glanced towards the house as

the phone rang. 'Valerie will answer that,' he added absent-mindedly. 'So you're saying that all these symptoms Sultan has could be caused by roundworm and not food poisoning after all?'

Hannah and Helen clung to every word.

'It's possible. Roundworm can cause serious problems, especially in a young horse like Sultan. For instance, it can block the arteries and cause internal bleeding. It often damages the liver and lungs too. And the first noticeable symptoms are a bit like colic; the horse gets short of breath and restless. He often staggers and collapses suddenly.'

'That's it!' Hannah cried. 'That's exactly what happened on Saturday!'

'What do we do?' Helen wanted to know. Suddenly everything had changed. There was hope that Sultan might not die.

'We put another tube into his stomach.' Sally Freeman took her bag from the car and strode towards the stable. 'This time we pump in something called anthelmintic to kill the parasite. Then we start him on a course of iron and vitamin B12 injections.'

Hannah ran after her. 'And will it cure him?' she demanded.

Mrs Freeman shrugged. 'If we haven't left it too late,' she muttered, asking Mr Saunders to follow her.

Helen closed her eyes and clasped her hands together. She stood for a moment, head tilted back. 'Make it all right!' she whispered. 'Make it so that Sultan gets better!'

But just then, before Helen and Hannah had time to follow Sally Freeman into the stable to watch her treat the patient, Valerie Saunders came running out of the house. She flew across the terrace, her face looking drained and shocked.

'Geoffrey!' She ran past the twins, hardly seeing them. 'Where are you?'

Mr Saunders paused in the stable doorway. He turned. 'I'm here. What is it?'

'It's the school. The headteacher is on the phone. Oh, Geoffrey – Laura's run away!'

Eight

'Don't worry,' the Nesfield police told Mr and Mrs Saunders when they heard the full story. 'Your daughter will probably head straight home to see this sick horse of hers.'

'Laura's bound to come back to Doveton,' Luke Martin told David Moore across the counter of the village shop. 'She must have panicked when the twins let the news about Sultan slip. She would only have one idea in her head, and that would be to get back here to see him as soon as she could.'

The whole village knew about Laura's sudden disappearance.

Miss Wesley announced it to her class in registration. 'I want you to listen very carefully. Put your hand up if you know Laura Saunders from Doveton Manor.'

A forest of hands shot up, including Hannah's and Helen's. Their mum had made them come to school, even after the news had broken and Mr and Mrs Saunders had learned how the twins hadn't been able to keep the secret of Sultan's illness after all. But they sat miserably at the back of the class, staring out of the window as the teacher went on.

'Well, Laura has gone missing from her boarding-school and her parents have brought in the police to look for her. They want us all to help.'

'Miss, what should we do?' Sam Lawson from Crackpot Farm jumped up, ready to rush out and start a search party.

'Calm down, Sam. All we want you to do is to keep your eyes open. If you do see Laura when you're out in the playground, or on your way home after school, what you must do is go straight home and tell a grown-up who can telephone the police straight away.'

'Why, Miss? Won't she go home if she gets this far?' Sam thought she would just march up the drive of Doveton Manor and in through the big front door.

'Not if she's run away from school. She might think she's in too much trouble and want to hide.'

Sam's eyes lit up again. 'So if we see her, we're not to say anything to scare her off. We just tell the police and they go and pick her up.'

'Exactly, Sam. And you must be very sensible about this. Laura's parents are worried about her. They don't want her to be hitching lifts to get back home, or staying out in the open all night. That would be dangerous.'

At the back of the room, Helen clenched her fists. Hannah scrunched her eyes shut. This was all their fault!

As Miss Wesley asked the class to get out their geography books and begin work, the twins sat horrified by what they'd done.

'Hannah, Helen!' Miss Wesley came and leaned over their shoulders. She spoke quietly.

They started out of their daze. Helen jumped up to fetch their books from the drawer.

'No, I don't want you to start work.' The teacher drew them both to the front of the class and out into the corridor. 'I've had a message asking you to go to the office,' she explained with a look of serious concern. 'Mr Saunders is here with a policewoman from Nesfield. They want to talk to you about a phone call Laura made last night.'

Hannah's heart thumped. Helen gasped.

'I'm sure there's no need to worry,' Miss Wesley said kindly. 'I expect they want to make sure that they have every last scrap of information.' She sent them along quickly, before they had time to think.

And there in the school entrance hall was the tall figure of Mr Saunders, next to a young, curly-haired policewoman, who stood holding her hat, reading the noticeboard. They turned as the twins approached.

'The first thing we need to know is exactly why Laura decided to run away,' the policewoman said, once she'd sorted out Helen from Hannah and sat them on chairs inside the office. 'You were the last people she spoke to. When she came off the phone from talking to you about Sultan, she

didn't say a word to anyone in school. They say she was upset, but no one could find out what was wrong. She went to bed early. Then sometime in the middle of last night, she must have climbed out through the window of her room, which is in a modern block of dormitories facing the games field. No one saw her go, so we don't know what time this was.'

Hannah pictured what had happened; while she and Helen lay awake the night before, staring out at the moon, listening to the wind in the tree, Laura had been planning her escape. She probably went to bed with her clothes on, a packed bag hidden under her bed . . .

'We think she may have had a bit of money with her, but not much,' the policewoman went on. 'We don't know whether she would catch a train or a bus, or if she would try to hitch a lift.'

Helen thought of Laura creeping out of her room in the middle of the night. Where would she have gone? What would she have done, faced with the pitch-blackness . . . ?

'We're very sorry,' Hannah whispered, staring at the floor. She didn't dare to meet Mr Saunders' gaze.

'No. It's my fault.' He spoke for the first time. Helen stared. Hannah held on to her seat with both hands. 'I blame myself. It was my idea not to tell her about Sultan. It put you two in an impossible position. I'm the one who should be sorry.'

'You're not angry?' Hannah asked.

'Only with myself. If I'd taken proper care of the horse, he would never have fallen ill in the first place. And I shouldn't have asked you two to cover up the truth either. No, I'm the one who's completely to blame!'

'And we need your help,' the policewoman added. 'We want you to tell us exactly what Laura said when she spoke to you last night.'

'Did she tell you what she was planning to do?' Geoffrey Saunders asked eagerly.

Helen shook her head. 'Not me.'

'Nor me.' All Hannah remembered was the phone going dead.

'And what did you tell her?' The policewoman turned back to Helen.

'Not much. Laura thought Sultan must have fallen, but I said he hadn't.'

'Then Helen handed the phone to me, and by this time Laura was really worried. She didn't believe Helen, so she asked me again if he'd had an accident. She thought he had fallen and that it was so bad he had to be put down.'

'She thought Sultan was dead?' Mr Saunders echoed.

Hannah and Helen nodded.

'This makes thing worse,' the policewoman said quietly. 'If she thinks that's the case, why would she bother coming home at all, poor girl?'

'She could be anywhere!' her father admitted.

'I'd better let my sergeant know.' Putting her hat on firmly, the policewoman thanked the twins and led the way out of the office.

'The whole school is going to be looking for Laura,' Helen told Mr Saunders. She'd seen his face grow grimmer and his head had sunk forward.

'And we'll ride Solo up on to the fell after school today,' Hannah decided. 'We know all Laura and Sultan's favourite places. Maybe that's where she's decided to go.'

He nodded and thanked them. 'And you'll visit Sultan?'

'Would you like us to?'

Another nod. 'Sally Freeman says he still needs all the care and attention he can get if he's going to pull through. And he's very fond of you two. A visit could do him the world of good.'

'We'll come straight after school,' Hannah told him.

Helen nodded. She felt sorry for the whole Saunders family and the mess they were in. 'We won't let Sultan down!' she promised.

*

'Sally says there's been a slight improvement,' Valerie Saunders told the twins. She went with them to the stable, to where Sultan lay resting in his stall.

'He does look a bit better,' Helen whispered.

The horse raised his head and snickered as they went in. His dark eyes were less dull, he seemed pleased to see them.

'He's been an absolute angel,' Mrs Saunders told them. 'Even when he has those horrible tubes down his throat he doesn't make any fuss.'

'And all those jabs must be nasty too.' Hannah knelt beside him and stroked his cheek. 'You've been a brave boy, Sultan!'

Valerie Saunders sighed. 'Not a murmur from him, ever since he collapsed. You wouldn't think he was the same horse as before!' She stood, arms folded, looking sadly down. 'If only Laura knew!'

Hannah and Helen didn't have to ask if there was any news of the runaway. They could tell by the strained look on her mum's face that there wasn't, so they kept their visit short; told Sultan what a great patient he was, how he must take the tablets the vet gave him.

'They'll make you well again,' Hannah whispered, scratching his head and stroking his ears.

'Then we'll build you up with lovely sweet hay,' Helen promised.

'And oats, and bran-mash and carrots!' Hannah added.

Helen remembered their own Solo's favourite treat. 'And rosy-red apples.'

'Then, before you know it, we'll be able to take you up on Doveton Fell with Solo,' Hannah added.

Sultan turned his head to follow the twins as they backed away towards the door. For a few moments, it looked as if he was going to struggle to his feet and totter after them. But he tried, failed, and sank back on to his side.

'Still no sign of Laura Saunders?' Luke Martin called when Hannah and Helen rode by later that evening.

Hannah didn't stop pedalling. 'Not yet!' She flew by on her bike, gathering speed for the steep slope up the lane on to Doveton Fell.

Helen trotted by on Solo, with Speckle at their heels. 'We're out looking now!' she told him.

'Like all the rest of the village.' Luke told her he'd scoured the cricket pitch and pavilion, and the fields behind. 'If Doveton is where she headed, it's only a matter of time before someone sees her!'

'We hope!' Helen said goodbye to Luke, went on after Hannah and caught her up. 'Luke says everyone in Doveton is looking for Laura,' she told her. 'The problem is, Laura must know it. She's bound to keep her head down until after it gets dark.'

'If she's got any sense,' Hannah agreed. 'But she might be lying low up on the fell. I still think it's worth having a look.'

They both nodded and went on.

'If this is where she's hiding, she must be getting cold by now.' Hannah had left her bike by an old stile and gone on across the ferns and heather on foot, heading for the ridge. She zipped her jacket as the wind got up, seeing Speckle reach the top of the hill before them.

'At least we'll get a good view from up here.' Helen urged Solo on. He felt solid and sure as he overtook Hannah and tackled the track across the final scree slope.

'What can you see?' Hannah gasped as she joined them on the ridge.

'Lakes and mountains,' Helen replied flatly. 'Empty space. No Laura.' From the saddle, she looked down into the next valley, along the high tracks, back down towards Doveton.

Hannah sighed. 'Worth a try.' She looked near by, behind rocks, in among the ancient oak trees that grew on the sheltered side of the ridge.

Speckle joined the search, sniffing round the roots, following scents, trotting back to begin again.

In the end, Helen gave in and turned Solo towards home. 'Laura's too clever to give herself away even if she is somewhere near.'

Reluctantly Hannah agreed. Dusk was drawing in, stealing the light from the lower slopes. The vanishing sun glowed pink on the western hills. 'Unless she waits until after dark,' she said suddenly.

Helen reined Solo back. 'And then comes out of hiding to visit Sultan when no one's around!' Of course!

'That's what we would do.'

'Make sure everyone was in bed . . .'

'. . . Wait until well after midnight . . .' Hannah whispered.

'. . . Then when it was completely quiet . . .'

'. . . And all the lights were off and no one was moving . . .'

Helen knew that this was the way they would do it if they were in Laura's position and they feared that their own horse was dying or dead. '. . . We'd creep into Sultan's stable to see for ourselves!'

Nine

'What was that?' Hannah sat bolt upright in bed. The alarm clock on her shelf said half-past four.

Helen was already out of bed and at the window. 'I don't know. Speckle must have heard something!' He'd come and poked his nose against her sleeping face until she woke up.

From his basket at the foot of Hannah's bed, Scruffy whined softly. Hannah got out and stroked him. 'Shh!' she warned, as she went to join Helen at the window. 'Can you see anything?'

'No.' The farmyard below was quiet and still, except for silent shadows flickering under the giant tree by the gate. 'But look at Speckle; he definitely thinks there's something down there!'

Their dog had his paws on the window ledge and his tail was wagging furiously.

'Why isn't he barking?' Hannah knew he would usually make a lot of noise. 'If there's someone creeping around down there, why isn't he warning the whole house?' She kept her own voice to a faint whisper as she peered into the shadows.

'Maybe he recognised who it was!' Helen whispered back. She turned to stare at Hannah.

'Laura!' they said together, almost as if they'd been expecting her.

Speckle wagged his tail until they thought it would drop off.

'It is!' Hannah felt sure.

'Let's go!' Helen slipped her feet into her trainers and darted to the door. 'Shh!' she warned Speckle again. The dog's hard claws had rattled on the floorboards as he ran after her. From his basket, Scruffy gave a short, sharp yap, then jumped out and hobbled after them.

'Don't wake Mum and Dad!' Hannah decided to carry Scruffy downstairs.

The cold night air hit them as Helen threw open the kitchen door and stepped outside. The breeze cut through her thin pyjamas. She waited for Hannah to put Scruffy down and ease the door closed behind them, then they all made warily for the gate, where the shadows were darkest.

Speckle trotted ahead. He disappeared behind the rabbit hutch, the white flash of his tail bobbing mysteriously. Scruffy, pale and ghostly in the dim moonlight, limped after him.

Helen clutched Hannah's arm. 'Did you see that?'

'No. What?'

'Over there, behind the wall. I saw something move!'

'Laura?' Hannah called softly.

No answer. Scruffy reached the wall and saw Speckle leap easily from ground to wall-top. He whimpered as he put his full weight on his injured paw.

'Wait here!' Helen ordered. She climbed the wall, saw a figure crouched behind it, muffled in a dark jacket and trousers.

Speckle gave a pleased wag of his tail and

trotted towards the crouching figure. Hannah followed Helen over the wall. 'Laura, thank heavens!' She jumped into the long grass at the side of the road and stumbled after the others.

But Scruffy hated being left behind in the farmyard. He scrabbled at the wall and whined.

'Hush, Scruffy!' Helen hissed. She saw the figure in the shadows stand up, saw her jacket hood fall back, recognised the long, fair hair and pale, anxious features.

Scruffy ignored the command. He yapped, then barked. From deep in his throat he let off a volley of sound that ripped through the silence.

Laura shied away at the noise. She pushed Speckle off and turned to run.

'Wait! It's OK!' Hannah began.

A light went on in their mum and dad's bedroom. The window opened as Scruffy went on tearing the quiet night apart. In the field behind the house, Solo's hooves thudded nearer; in the henhouse in the yard, the chickens scuttled and fluttered.

And Laura took fright. Without waiting for an explanation, she ran away, stumbling through the grass, out of the shadow of the chestnut tree, down the lane towards the village.

'Wait!' By now Hannah was desperate. If only Laura would listen. She set off after her. 'It's OK! Wait, Laura!'

Helen glanced back at the house. She saw her dad leave the window, saw other lights come on downstairs. He was on his way to sort Scruffy out. There was no time to think, no time to stop and explain. The only thing that mattered was to head Laura off and tell her the truth about Sultan.

'I've lost her!' Hannah cried, as Helen joined her in the lane by the entrance to High Hartwell. 'She cut across the fields!'

'Where's Speckle?'

'He went with her.' They climbed the stile and ran through the wet grass. Fred Hunt's herd of black and white cows stood still as statues, watching them sprint across the meadow.

'If only Scruffy had kept quiet!' Hannah sighed.

'I wonder how long she'd been waiting out there.'

'Poor thing!'

'Look, here's Speckle!' Helen saw him trotting back up the hill. He came right up, then turned, urging them to hurry after him. 'That's a good boy, show us where Laura's gone!'

'Home,' Hannah muttered. 'I bet anything!' Now that she'd been spotted, it was the only thing she could do. Since she hadn't been able to discover from the twins what was going on, she would head straight for Doveton Manor and find out for herself.

And sure enough, Speckle kept his nose to the ground, leading them across Fred Hunt's fields, down into the valley, with the lake gleaming in the distance and all the houses of Doveton standing silent and dark.

A dog barked at the gate of Lakeside Farm.

'That's Ben!' Helen hissed. There was no one around, no cars, no lights on, but the darkness made her whisper.

Speckle led them on, skirting round John Fox's farm, past Miss Wesley's cottage by the lake, on to the main street.

'There she is!' Hannah caught sight of a figure cutting behind Luke Martin's shop. 'She's taking the public footpath across to the Manor!'

Speckle saw her too and raced ahead.

'What shall we do?' Helen needed a plan. Laura was too far ahead for them to catch her before she reached home. They couldn't warn her about Sultan; she would find him in the stable too weak to stand, looking dangerously ill.

Hannah shook her head. 'Just follow her!' she gasped.

The outline of Doveton Manor loomed up ahead, across the last fields, through the empty paddock. Its tall windows were blank, the blinds drawn. In the stable yard the neat white doors stood out against the dark stone.

Sultan's door swung open as the twins ran across his paddock. Speckle came padding back towards them.

Together they crossed the paved yard, approached the stable and peered inside.

'Oh, Sultan! Oh, you poor thing!' Laura fell to her knees beside her sick horse. Her fair hair had escaped from its band and fell across her face as she put her arms round Sultan's neck and sobbed. 'Oh, thank heavens you're still alive. But what's happened to you?'

He turned his head towards her and nosed at her shoulder, his dark mane straggled across his forehead and falling limply down his neck.

'Sultan, I'm here now. Everything's going to be all right. Please don't leave me!' Laura begged.

Helen started forward with tears in her own eyes. 'It's OK, Laura,' she whispered. 'Sultan's got roundworm. We're treating him to make him better!' She saw Sultan heave himself sideways and struggle on to his knees as Laura sank back into the straw.

Hannah went to help him stand. 'Look!' she whispered to Laura.

Slowly, shakily Sultan got to his feet. The straw rustled and stuck to his dull, sweating flanks, he flicked his tail, shook his head and made a supreme effort.

'You can do it!' Helen urged.

He tried again. He was up and standing, swaying from side to side, but determined.

Staring and shaking her head, Laura stood up too. She put out her hand to steady him. 'Good boy!' she whispered, seeing that he'd made the

effort specially for her. 'Brave boy!'

Helen and Hannah watched the two of them together, Laura with her arms round the horse's neck, her head pressed against him, Sultan with his head up, trembling but dead set on showing them that come what may he was going to make it.

Hannah brushed her tears away and smiled. 'The treatment must be working!' she whispered.

Helen nodded. 'Sultan's going to live after all!'

As dawn crept into the spring sky, the Moores and the Saunders gathered in the stables at Doveton Manor.

David Moore had discovered Scruffy whining and barking alone in the yard at Home Farm. Mary Moore found the twins' beds empty and Speckle missing from his basket. Quickly they'd realised what was happening and followed Hannah and Helen down into the valley.

They drove up to the Manor just as Laura was reunited with her beloved horse. More lights had gone on; this time in the big house, at the sound of the Moores' car coming up the drive.

And now; after the whys and wherefores, the saying sorry and all being forgiven, the really important things could be done.

'Sultan, you look a mess!' Laura told him briskly. She slipped a headcollar over his ears and gently led him out of his stall.

'I'll muck out!' Hannah offered, rushing to fetch the fork and brush. She heaped the old straw into a barrow, swept the floor, and spread a new layer of straw from the bale for Sultan's day-bed.

'I'll bring the brushes and combs!' Helen volunteered.

'You need a thorough grooming!' Laura told him. 'We'll soon have you looking handsome again!'

They worked with picks and brushes, prising out dried mud and tiny pebbles from Sultan's hooves, then tackling his dull coat with dandy-brush and body-brush, with rubber and curry-comb.

'That's better!' Laura stood back and took a deep breath. The thoroughbred's coat gleamed like new horse chestnuts.

Then Hannah started on his dark mane,

brushing it through a few strands at a time until they were knot-free and she could lay them neatly to one side. 'Not long now,' she murmured, as Sultan shifted slightly. 'You're being very good!'

'He looks a different animal!' Mr Saunders had watched in silence, but now he nodded and walked all round the horse. He put his arm round Laura's shoulder. 'Sally Freeman will hardly recognise him when she gets here for her morning visit.'

Laura smiled. 'Do you think we should rug him?'

He nodded. 'Leg bandages wouldn't be a bad idea either. They'll keep him warm.'

So there was more for the twins and Laura to do before they finally led Sultan back into his stall, tied up a new haynet for him to nibble at, and poured fresh water into his bucket.

Meanwhile, the grown-ups thought ahead.

'You see how Sultan has perked up since Laura's been here,' Valerie Saunders said quietly. 'I know the vet's new treatment put him back on the right road, and Hannah and Helen have been absolutely brilliant, but I'm sure it was seeing Laura again that has made all the difference!'

Sultan nuzzled hay from Laura's palm.

'Hmm.' Geoffrey Saunders agreed. 'I think she'd better stick around till after the weekend. She can go back to school next week.'

As Helen and Hannah put the brushes and combs back in place, they grinned secretly across the bench.

Laura stroked Sultan's dark, velvety nose.

'In fact, Laura, I think it would be a good idea if you came home every weekend until the end of term,' Mr Saunders told her. 'Getting him completely better is going to be a long process, and having you around is going to be good for him. Mind you, you'll still have to keep up with your schoolwork during the week.'

'I'll work extra hard.' She smiled, nodded, and put her head against Sultan's smooth cheek.

Hannah grinned and stuck up both her thumbs. Helen whispered a silent 'Yeah!'

'Talking of school, it's time to get you two ready!' Mary Moore brought them back to earth with a bump.

'Oh, Mu-um!' Hannah complained.

'Do we have to?' Helen pleaded.

Their dad looked them up and down, from the straw in their dark fringes to their splashed striped pyjamas and their soggy trainers. 'Unless you want to go to school dressed like that!' he said with eyebrows raised.

'Oh, Da-ad!' they said together.

But there was nothing for it; they would have to leave Laura and her parents to get on with nursing the patient.

'When he's strong enough we'll take him out on the fell again with Solo!' Helen promised.

'If you want us to!' Hannah added.

They stood in the yard, reluctant to leave.

Laura nodded. She'd taken off her jacket and tied her hair back, ready to clean up the paddock. 'He'll need loads of work to get him back into condition.'

'Solo loves having Sultan with us.' Helen pictured them up on the ridge, the wind in the horses' manes, the sky blue, the white blossom in the valley below . . .

'So do Speckle and Scruffy,' Hannah told her. They were a brilliant foursome; the sturdy grey pony, the handsome chestnut thoroughbred, the speedy Speckle and the rough-and-tumble mongrel Scruffy.

'Sultan loves it too,' Laura told them. 'And I've a feeling he's going to be a whole lot easier to handle when he gets over this illness!'

'Not so bossy,' Hannah agreed. She glanced back into the quiet stable, where Sultan picked at his hay and munched steadily.

'I don't care!' Helen said. 'He can be as head-strong as he likes, just so long as we get him up there again!'

They all nodded at that.

'We will!' Laura promised.

And from the peaceful shadows of his fresh, clean stall, the patient stamped his feet. 'We will!' he seemed to echo with a defiant toss of his beautiful head.

Another Hodder Children's book

SORREL THE SUBSTITUTE
Home Farm Twins 12

Jenny Oldfield

Meet Helen and Hannah. They're identical twins – and mad about the animals on their Lake District farm!

Helen and Hannah look after Sage, the school rabbit, during the holidays. But he gives them the slip. When their teacher, Miss Wesley, plans a visit to Home Farm, the twins borrow Sorrel, an identical rabbit, to fool her. Will the trick work? And can the twins find Sage before he comes to harm?

SKYE THE CHAMPION
Home Farm Twins 13

Jenny Oldfield

Meet Helen and Hannah. They're identical twins – and mad about the animals on their Lake District farm!

When their dad is involved in a car accident, the twins are glad he's not hurt. But the trailer he hit was carrying a prize highland cow and her calf – and the young calf is injured. Will the angry owner sue Mr Moore? Can Helen and Hannah find a way to take the now unwanted calf off his hands?

SUGAR & SPICE THE PICKPOCKETS
Home Farm Twins 14

Jenny Oldfield

Meet Helen and Hannah. They're identical twins – and mad about the animals on their Lake District farm!

Two squirrels invade the loft of the local shop and cause a row in Doveton. Should they be left alone or got rid of? When small items vanish from the shop, it seems as though the squirrels' days are numbered. But Hannah and Helen suspect that someone or something else is beyond the thefts – and they plan to investigate!

Another Hodder Children's book

SOPHIE THE SHOW-OFF
Home Farm Twins 15

Jenny Oldfield

Meet Helen and Hannah. They're identical twins – and mad about the animals on their Lake District farm!

Sophie's a rescue cat with a habit of showing off – and it's causing all sorts of problems! Parading by the lake in front of tourists, she slips off the ferry rail; stalking doves on the shop roof, she nearly takes a tumble. Luckily for her, the twins are on hand to help. But now Sophie plans to put in an appearance at the local cricket match! Can Helen and Hannah stop her?

HOME FARM TWINS
Jenny Oldfield

66127 5	Speckle The Stray	£3.50	❏
66128 3	Sinbad The Runaway	£3.50	❏
66129 1	Solo The Homeless	£3.50	❏
66130 5	Susie The Orphan	£3.50	❏
66131 3	Spike The Tramp	£3.50	❏
66132 1	Snip and Snap The Truants	£3.50	❏
68990 0	Sunny The Hero	£3.50	❏
68991 9	Socks The Survivor	£3.50	❏
68992 7	Stevie The Rebel	£3.50	❏
68993 5	Samson The Giant	£3.50	❏
70399 7	Scruffy The Scamp	£3.50	❏
69983 3	Sultan the Patient	£3.50	❏

All Hodder Children's books are available at your local bookshop or newsagent, or can be ordered direct from the publisher. Just tick the titles you want and fill in the form below. Prices and availability subject to change without notice.

Hodder Children's Books, Cash Sales Department, Bookpoint, 39 Milton Park, Abingdon, OXON, OX14 4TD, UK. If you have a credit card you may order by telephone – (01235) 400414.

Please enclose a cheque or postal order made payable to Bookpoint Ltd to the value of the cover price and allow the following for postage and packing:
UK & BFPO – £1.00 for the first book, 50p for the second book, and 30p for each additional book ordered up to a maximum charge of £3.00.
OVERSEAS & EIRE – £2.00 for the first book, £1.00 for the second book, and 50p for each additional book.

Name ....

Address ....

....

....

If you would prefer to pay by credit card, please complete:
Please debit my Visa/Access/Diner's Card/American Express (delete as applicable) card no:

Signature ....

Expiry Date ....